Fire Light Cabin Bright

a Firehawks romance story
by
M. L. Buchman

Buchman Bookworks

Other works by M.L. Buchman

Where Dreams Reside
Maria's Christmas Table
Where Dreams Unfold
Where Dreams Are Written

Dieties Anonymous

Cookbook from Hell: Reheated
Saviors 101

Thrillers

Swap Out!
One Chef!
Two Chef!

SF/F Titles

Nara
Monk's Maze

1

Just as some days are hotter than others, some fires are hotter than others. And the Checker Mill Fire was a scorcher.

Tori Ellison checked her watch but couldn't see it. Even shining her helmet headlamp on it didn't really help. Her eyes were lack-of-sleep sore and they stung from smoke and salty sweat. She couldn't taste anything but that salt and the char that it collected as it dribbled down her face; the peanut and dark chocolate flavor of her energy bar hadn't lasted more than a few minutes before being overwhelmed.

She'd volunteered to scout what lay over the next ridge while the rest of her Hotshot fire crew crashed out for an hour. She was supposed to go ten minutes out and ten back, but couldn't seem to focus on the watch to tell how long she'd been gone. Three minutes? Fifteen? She no longer knew.

It was zero-dark-thirty, like the military guys said, which was all that really mattered.

Where was here? She wasn't so sure of that either.

She was always doing dumb, impulsive things like this. In college one of her nicknames had been the Energizer Bunny because she'd never had the sense to stop until she dropped. The Bunny part had been shed after she'd punched a particularly obnoxious frat boy hard enough to shatter his nose.

When Tori hit the fire line, her new firefighter nickname was Ginger within three days.

It wasn't that her hair was red—she was a bob-cut blond. The crew chief, Candace Cantrell, had grown up with a Labrador named Ginger who also never knew when to stop.

A low-hanging Douglas fir branch slapped in her face because she was too weary to step around it. At least it was green and smelled of life and fresh pine. She felt bolstered by its presence; it was standing in the cool forest night, trusting her and her team to save it from the encroaching wildfire.

Tori trudged by it and promised to do her best—trudged because trotting was long past her abilities at the moment. They'd come off the Bell Creek Fire along Washington's Skagit River less than forty-eight hours ago and now had been on the Checker Mill for the last thirty-six straight. The Cascade Mountains were rough and she normally liked the challenge… when she was conscious.

She crested the low ridge in a thick stand of trees. It would take a lot of cutting to clear a fire line here if they had to. Too tired to even dodge the branches, she raised her arms in front of her face and ploughed through the heart of the stand.

The trees gave way the moment before her feet snarled in thick vines and she face-planted on the ground.

Her radio crackled, "Ginger, check in."

"Yo, Candace." The ground was soft. Well-tilled soil cool against her cheek. She didn't waste extra effort trying to stand up. It felt so good to lie down, for even a moment.

"Report."

"Hard-ass," Tori teased her. Since it was something the Hotshot team's leader was proud of, it was a safe call. "Trees much thicker at the ridge. Eight to eighteen-inch diameter Doug fir. Can't see much else."

"Where are you now?"

"Lying on the ground," she looked around to try and be more specific, and was confronted by something large and green. Big enough to completely block her view. "In a zucchini patch."

"A residence?"

That would be bad news. Needing to defend a residence, or worse a neighborhood, could drastically change a fire attack plan.

"Ginger?"

"Hang on. Hang on. Sheesh!" Tori forced her arms beneath her and levered herself upward. They shook with the effort. She'd really tapped herself out this time; right out to the limits.

Once upright she twisted her head side to side to swing the headlamp around.

"I'm in a vegetable garden," she reported.

"You're in *my* vegetable garden, 'Ginger'," a deep male voice sounded from the dark.

She twisted the lamp around and found a mountain man standing about ten feet down a row of tomatoes. Except he wasn't hairy, messy, or clad in rotting animal skins. He wore gym shorts and a frown. She couldn't see his eyes because he had his arm raised to protect them from the glare of her lamp, but from the nose down was very fine. Not a six-pack ab guy, but no extra bits either.

"Who are you? And why were you eaves-dropping on my private conversation?"

"My name's Colin James. And if you're in my garden on the radio, how private can your conversation be?"

Tori hit the transmit key, "I'm in Colin's secret garden. And he's just as much of a know-it-all as the one in the book."

"If Dickon shows up, he's mine," Candace replied. "I always had a crush on Dickon."

Tori heard a soft *Hey!* in the background, probably Candace's husband Luke, a top member of the IHC crew.

"What are you doing in my squash?" the man asked from behind his raised arm.

"Well, that's no way to address a lady, Colin."

2

Her voice was the only thing that distinguished her as one. Colin had been lying out in the hammock watching the stars—it was too beautiful and warm a night to stay in his cabin—when he'd heard a hard grunt and rustle from his vegetable garden.

It had sounded human rather than ursine—he didn't worry about bears here… much. When he'd looked, there was a light shining low under his plants. Not stopping for shoes or a flashlight, he raced out to scare away the poacher. He'd put a lot of time and care into his garden and no midnight skulker was going to rob him.

He'd been stopped in his tracks by what he found. Between the zucchini and the pumpkins lay a fully clad firefighter, and one that was making no effort to get up.

By the reflected light off the nearby leaves, Colin had seen a hardhat that might have once been yellow under all the soot. The firefighter wore similarly colored jacket and pants, heavy boots, and a small pack. One hand clutched a nasty-looking axe and the other a handheld radio.

And then the firefighter had spoken and turned out to be a she. Named Ginger.

"If you're lying in my vegetables, I'll address you any way I choose. And get that light out of my eyes."

"Oh, sorry," she turned the lamp toward the ground.

He had a brief glimpse of an oval face and a hint of blond hair before she flicked it off and they were plunged into darkness. He blinked hard, but his night vision was shot and wouldn't be back for several minutes.

He couldn't see, but he could hear that she hadn't moved.

"Are you planning to just lie there all night among my veggies?"

She giggled. "You have a very comfortable garden." A firefighter who giggled.

"What are you doing here anyway?"

"Uh," Ginger paused. "I'm here because…" she sounded as if she was trying to figure that out for herself, "…oh, yeah. I'm here because there's a forest fire in the next valley over. I'm the scout."

Suddenly a dozen things he hadn't paid any real attention to earlier in the day made sense. He'd kept smelling wood smoke, but no one in their right mind would have their fireplace going on such a hot day. Besides, he was pretty sure that he had no neighbors for a long way in any direction.

Also there had been clouds to the north, but he hadn't really paid attention. The novel was finally going well and he hadn't been outside all day. Yet another reason he'd retired to the hammock with the sunset. Now though, he remembered that the clouds had been an odd color for a lightning storm, too dark.

There'd also been the sound of helicopters, but they were often used in logging operations. Maybe not so much today.

"How close?" he swallowed hard.

"A mile or so. I seem to have lost track."

"What kind of a firefighter are you?"

"An exhausted one."

"Here," he reached out into the dark. "Let me help you up."

Somehow they found each other's hands. But when he braced a foot forward to pull her up, he stepped barefoot right on a planting stake. He tumbled forward onto her with an exclamation on his part and a curse on hers.

"That's your idea of being helpful?" she grumbled from where she lay beneath him in the dark.

"Ginger, this is Candace," the radio squawked loudly in his ear. "Are we looking at an individual or a community? I don't show anything on the map."

He tried to roll off her, but the big zucchini bush stopped him. When he shifted the other direction, he partly rolled onto her fireaxe.

"Hey Candace. I can confirm an individual. Clumsy, but cute."

"I'm not—" Well, maybe he was being a klutz. But he hadn't exactly been prepared for a female firefighter lying on the dirt in his garden.

"Ginger!" The woman on the radio was sounding irritated.

"Hang on." Then Ginger reached up to assist him in getting off her, and clipped him fairly solidly on the jaw with a leather-gloved fist.

He tumbled into the vines.

"Oh crap. I'm sorry." She giggled again even as she groped around in the darkness, grabbed his arm for support, which pulled him back atop her with surprising strength. "Well, isn't that interesting."

This time when he tried to pull himself free, she pulled him down and kissed him. Hard.

3

What was she doing? Tori was deep in the kiss before any part of her brain woke up enough to be rational. The mostly unclad Colin was lying full upon her and, after a brief hesitation, was proving he was an exceptional kisser.

After enjoying the situation for several more moments, she managed a "Whoa." Then she pushed against his shoulders to shift him up and far enough away for her head to stop having ideas about where to go next with this mostly naked man. He tasted deliciously of male and toothpaste—a welcome relief from her own salt sweat and char—but it was dumb as could be for her to randomly kiss a total stranger.

Colin didn't resist as she pushed him back. Kept going until he was kneeling between her legs.

"Um," she had nothing to add to that. And she was almost tired enough to drag him back down on her.

"Ginger!"

"Spoilsport," she told the radio without keying the transmit key.

"She's persistent," Colin observed from nearby in the darkness. Her eyes had recovered enough to make out his outline against the stars.

"You have no idea. She needs to know…"

Something.

"I live alone here. Solo cabin. Is the fire coming my way?"

"Candace," somehow Tori had held onto the radio during the kiss. "It's a solo cabin of a man who tastes like mountain spring water."

"You kissed him?"

"Either I did or he did. I'm a little fuzzy on the details."

"Uh-huh," Candace wasn't buying it. "I'll send Luke up with a couple saws. Make sure the site is prepped for best defense. The fire has slowed and will be good until dawn. We'll get air attack to lay down a perimeter as soon as the helos are back aloft with the sunrise. Take an hour break."

"Roger that."

Now the question was, what to do with an hour?

4

On the gas camping stove, Colin had heated up the leftover chili he'd been planning to have for lunch tomorrow. The woman across the table was wolfing it down while it was still scalding hot as if she hadn't eaten in a week.

"Don't they feed you?"

"Only between fires. No time during a burn. You cook this?" She mumbled around a mouthful, halfway through the bowl.

"Yes, my chef is off this week."

"It's good," she drank back a glass of water in a single gulp. "Really good." She slowed down and began looking around the candlelit cabin. "I see the butler is off this week too."

He looked around and grimaced. "I'm not generally this messy." He was ten miles up a dead-end road and an hour-long hike on a steep trail past that. He hadn't exactly prepared for visitors. And it wasn't that bad. His sheets were still spread on the couch, his clothes piled on the chair, and the floor hadn't been swept in a while. But the dishes were clean and the food all stowed. His desk was a train wreck, but that was always the case when he was in the middle of writing a novel.

At least he'd taken a wash in the stream recently. Colin rubbed at his chin. Okay, should have shaved somewhere in the last few days, but how was he supposed to have known that he was going to have his first-ever visitor in five summers.

"You're not exactly all spic-and-span yourself," he told her.

She'd staggered into his cabin, dumping hardhat, jacket, and axe across the threshold. The cotton shirt she wore underneath was both sweat- and soot-stained. But it clung to her in amazing ways. The easy strength she'd revealed in the vegetable garden was evident in her athlete's shoulders. Her curves were feminine and sleek; as unlike his ex-wife as could be.

Mirella had been voluptuous…and needy as hell. The latter had made him feel the powerful protector at first, but what had started out as charming had become a cloying emptiness in the woman that could never be assuaged. He'd been on the verge of running and damn the expenses, when she'd decided to fill that emptiness with another man. He was still smarting from the whole mess—despite his lucky escape—and was not looking for another woman.

But looking *at* the woman before him was proving to be a pleasure.

"You're staring."

He was. "I am," he shrugged an apology. "You offer a lot to look at, Ginger." Her fitness, her curves, the face that would have looked merely nice on any lesser woman. Ginger's face was alive with emotion; smile or sarcasm, her feelings showed easily past the deep exhaustion.

"That's not my name."

"But on the radio…" he trailed off at her self-deprecating smile.

"Nickname I earned for being as dumb as a dog. Tori Ellison," she held out a hand and he shook it, "I never know when to quit."

"Easy answer, never."

5

Tori looked up at Colin sharply. It *was* the easy answer, but no one else ever understood that.

Hotshot crews were trained to keep going no matter what, right until the hallucinations of exhaustion set in, and she was still twenty-four hours from that state. But for everyone else, it was always a challenge to keep going. To push harder.

Instead, Tori always saw it as never having "quit" as an option. It made all the difference in the world, but she'd never been able to explain that to anyone satisfactorily.

"What makes you say that?" she asked carefully as she continued to eat the magnificent chili.

Colin looked around his cabin as if he'd stored the answer to her question somewhere in the room.

It was a sweet setup. A generous one-room; a mountain cabin without being primitive. Big windows that told of a magnificent southern view hidden by the darkness. They sat at a small table for two that might be more workbench than dining table. A hand pump at the sink spoke volumes. But there were also shelves of books, a cozy wood stove, and, perched at a desk cluttered with paper and books, sat a small laptop computer—the only sign of electricity in the whole cabin. She spotted the large battery and would bet that there was a solar panel somewhere outside that fed it. The laptop, she decided, was the focus of the room. The rest was disorganized, not because he was a slob—for the kitchen was immaculate—but because he didn't care.

He too had turned to the desk as if the answer was there somewhere but he couldn't see it. No. He saw it clearly, but wasn't sure about sharing it.

"Writer's cabin," she guessed.

He nodded, then froze like a animal wondering if it was too late to escape the fire.

"Published."

A very careful nod.

So, not a comfortable topic. Which meant he was either a total failure or a major success. If the former, the kitchen wouldn't be so neat…or the desk so messy; a failure would fail in multiple ways. So, a success that he didn't want to reveal, that had him living in a remote cabin with a vegetable garden.

She returned to her study of him rather than his cabin. Not a burden. Tori had thought he was good-looking by the light of her head lamp, but his arm had hidden his best feature. Warm brown eyes lively with a sharp brain behind them. A writer's brain. But they were also warm with emotion, and each time they drifted down her body, more and more heat was revealed there.

"I dated a writer once," she said without thinking first.

"I hate him already," Colin offered the comment amiably.

"He was okay. But he didn't understand about perseverance." Tori had learned enough while dating Andy to know that writing was all about perseverance. She could see that Colin was surprised she knew that reality.

"You're frustrating me at the moment," he remarked and it sounded like a topic change, so she let it be.

"Good. Only one thing this girl likes more than frustrating a handsome, successful man."

"What's that?"

And suddenly Tori was the one who wanted the topic change. She knew that she was far too tired if she'd let that slip out. She'd gotten into firefighting courtesy of a brief fling with a smokejumper. He'd been fun enough, but their brief foray into the wilderness had been life changing.

Tori had always like the outdoors. She'd earned dual degrees in botany and ecology before that trip. To hang with a group of firefighters deep in the wilderness had been an option she'd never thought of until she met the smokie in a bar. He'd offered the briefest glimpse of a life in that uncontemplated world of wildland firefighting.

She'd even found it easy to fall in with the typical firefighter talk once she became one. But there was still a woman with a dream who'd been born on that trip.

The smokie's bosses had been along on the trip, a pair of heli-aviation pilots. A man and woman and their little daughter. Neither spoke much, but their unity—their perfect togetherness—had been such a daunting vision, that it had set the bar impossibly high. She wanted what they had.

Candace and Luke were another couple that felt that way—the only other example she'd ever met.

So, she trained and became a hotshot. On the teams she laughed and teased, and occasionally played the "I fight wildfires for a living" card to pick up a handsome man in a bar. But there was a part of her that dreamed of finding that "right man" someday.

That was the thing that this girl wanted more than frustrating a handsome, successful man.

Not a chance she'd be admitting that out loud though.

6

Colin watched her sleep.

He'd offered the couch, but she didn't want to mess it up with her soot-stained clothes. Instead, she landed in his back-porch hammock and was out in seconds. He parked himself in an Adirondack chair on the back porch and again took in the night.

The stars that he'd been watching to the east, were blocked to the west—the direction Tori had arrived from—by dark clouds. They weren't black, as clouds usually were at night, but glowed red along the bottoms as if they still caught the last of the long-past sunset.

Fire. They glowed red with fire. The hints of wood smoke from this morning were more constant, though still swirled aside by the gentle night breezes. Close, but not too close. Staying far away, he hoped.

He should go inside. Pack his notes and laptop in a bag so that he could grab it and go if he had to. But he couldn't break the easy comfort of sitting and watching Tori sleep.

The charge on his body guaranteed that any chance of sleep for himself lay a long way off. Pretty, motivated, tenacious, and smart were only a few of the adjectives he cataloged on her behalf. She'd synthesized what he was all about with very few clues, and then had the decency to read that he didn't want to talk about it.

Mirella, despite being the one who'd cheated on him, had wanted a big piece of who he was when she left. She wanted rights to any books he'd written while they were together and any number of other things that his attorney had refused to give up. By the time the acrimonious battle was complete, Colin had paid her nothing and she had convinced him that the only reason she'd ever been with him had been avarice. He liked to think that hadn't been the case. But however it had started, it had nothing to do with love.

He wondered what Tori was like when she wasn't drugged with exhaustion. Still beautiful. Still thoughtful. Still tenacious. He was surprised that he'd very much like to discover more despite swearing off women.

Colin knew too little to make conjectures, but he had enjoyed every waking moment they'd had together, at the table and even lying in the garden's dirt.

That kiss. That brief, spectacular kiss. That had been one thing about Mirella, the sex with her was always fantastic. She might have needed something he couldn't supply to send her seeking another man's bed, but the woman had been built hot and made to last.

He'd kissed Tori for approximately three seconds, and it washed any lingering, lonely-night fantasies of Mirella right out of his mind. If kissing Tori was that good, what would the rest of it be like?

"Been alone in the woods too long," he told the night quietly.

Colin came to the mountain cabin to write. To get away from people and the city and the distractions. He'd been seriously considering wintering over this year despite the harsh winters that sometimes swept the heights of the Cascades. Mirella had come to the cabin once, and departed rapidly. He'd guess that if he chose to winter over, Tori would be right there with him. And loving it.

He watched over her until a small light came bobbing toward him through the darkness. A tall man wearing a headlamp came up to the porch, flashed his light on Tori's sleeping face and then a quick scan around—without blinding Colin—before dousing the light.

"Name's Luke," the man stepped forward and offered a hand. His shake was strong, firefighter strong.

"Colin."

"She actually looks sweet when she's asleep," Luke commented.

"How about when she's awake?"

"Still sweet," Luke chuckled. "Telling you, something's gotta be wrong with the woman to be so consistently pleasant and cheery, but I haven't found it yet. She's a born firefighter. Thanks for watching over her, not that this one needs it."

"What does she need?"

7

Tori would have to pay Luke back for the "sweet" wisecrack.

"Don't think it's my place to be giving away any of the lady's secrets," Luke was telling Colin. "Why? You got an interest?"

Tori lay very still and awaited the answer.

"Might."

Colin *might* have an interest? All she'd done was punched him, kissed him… spectacularly, eaten his chili, and passed out in his hammock for an hour. She was about to rouse herself, despite how comfortable she was feeling, and give these two a quick whack with an axe handle just for being so male, when Luke finally replied.

"If you want to find a better person than Victoria Ellison, you're too late; I already married her. My Candace." Then Luke slapped her on the calf. "Rise and shine, Ginger. We've got some trees to trim. You're first up swamping."

Tori made a groan for Luke's benefit. When cutting line, one person was the sawyer, and the other hauled everything they cut as far from the fire line as possible. They'd switch off after every tank of fuel, but going from nice soft hammock to swamping was a rude awakening.

But Luke's compliment was high praise indeed; he was crazy about Candace and deservedly so.

She didn't know that Luke thought that highly of her as well.

Luke tramped off toward the trees.

Tori waited a moment by Colin, wishing she could see him better.

"Thanks for taking me in," she didn't know what else to say.

"You're welcome any time," he sounded surprised at this own words.

Whether she was unwilling to risk another supercharged, mega-turbo kiss, or the hour's sleep had been sufficient for her common sense to return, she merely shook his hand and turned for the trees.

He *might* have an interest?

It was stupid. It was based on nothing at all.

The only problem she could think of was that she *might* be having an interest as well.

8

Colin brewed coffee, pulled on boots and work clothes, and headed up the slope to join them. He did pack his grab bag and leave it inside the door just in case.

The coffee was taken, appreciated, and drunk while still too hot.

Tori, who was running the chain saw by the time he arrived, didn't even shut off the saw when she knocked her coffee back like a drug, then returned the mug with the briefest of nods. He almost didn't recognize her in the soft pre-dawn light. For one thing, she was back in her full helmet and gear. But also, she was in Ginger-mode. She was moving full tilt and nothing was going to break her focus. He knew that feeling and did his best not to feel rejected by her lack of acknowledgement.

She had cleats on her boots and a heavy belt that wrapped around the fir. She scaled up the tree to the lowest dead branches, then nipped them off with the saw. Moving the belt higher, the next dead branches dropped to the ground. In moments she was fifty feet in the air and a thick pile of dead branches had accumulated around the base of the tree.

Luke was at the prior tree, gathering up the dead branches and dragging them in the direction of the cabin. Douglas firs grew tall, and the lower branches often died off, yet still hung on for years.

Colin grabbed a bundle of branches and followed Luke. Luke had found the cliff edge below the cabin and dumped the branches over which then tumbled to the bottom. Even if they somehow caught fire there, all they'd do was scorch some rock. Colin pitched his load over.

They walked back together.

"I don't get what we're doing."

"Ladder fuels," Luke replied. "Fire wants to burn and climb up a tree. Get rid of undergrowth and it has less to burn, stays cooler on the ground. Cut away the deadwood and it has nothing to climb. The real problem happens when it reaches the crown. Hard to fight a crown fire from the ground."

With two of them swamping, they made quick work of what had already been cut.

Luke fired up a second saw and began clearing the undergrowth. Colin couldn't keep up with both of them, but whenever Tori or Luke ran out of fuel, they'd help him catch up as part of their refueling. Mid-morning he knew trouble was coming when a tanker plane roared by low overhead and dumped a broad swath of retardant on the trees. For a quarter mile, the big jet plane sent down a shower of the dark red liquid in an impossibly dense downpour.

Tori arrived beside him as the tanker finished the run and turned back for its next load. "Retardant coats the wood and keeps the oxygen from reaching it. No oxygen means no fire."

"Then what have we been doing here?" Colin waved at the trees, at the whole area they'd been parking-out.

"Layers of defense, like chapters in a book. Chapter One, we have a fireline cut about a half mile back. We're hoping to narrow the blaze, maybe even knock it out of the crown because it's running high and hot at the moment. Chapter Two, hopefully most of it dies when it hits the retardant line. Chapter Three, if we can really slow it down here, it won't do much more than mow the grass in your meadow before we can extinguish it. End of story."

He'd been right about smart and kind. She'd thought to switch her words into his metaphor to make sure he understood it easily, rather than assuming he could cross to her side of the fence.

"And if all three chapters fail? What's the fourth?" He'd miss his cabin. He'd rebuild, but there were a lot of good memories here; he could hear the stories that had been written in this idyllic spot.

She pointed up at the sky.

A small helicopter painted black with red flames came pounding up the hill. They watched it together as it flew over his cabin, a huge, bright-orange bucket on a cable dangled far below. The pilot didn't even slow down, just released the load of water dead-center on his roof. It soaked down the shingles and poured off the eaves in a waves.

"That's the epilogue, just in case the fire didn't get the message or tries to throw a few hot embers your way."

Colin could see it clearly. All of the different pieces and how they fit together as neatly as any story.

But he couldn't stop looking at the quietly competent woman he'd been working beside all morning.

"Just in case I don't get a chance to say it later, I meant what I said. You're welcome anytime."

9

Tori didn't know wat she was doing. It was her first break in weeks. The fire season was running hot and heavy, but Candace had finally declared that enough was enough and shuttered the Leavenworth Hotshots for five days. Thirty days without a break, they were all so punchy that safety was becoming an issue.

Tori had thought about hanging out in town like usual. But she didn't want the noise and the bars. She wanted the quiet that a smokejumper had introduced her to an age ago.

By the time she parked her battered Toyota pickup beside the shiny Jeep Wrangler, Tori at least knew her destination. As if she hadn't looked up the access road on a topo map the moment she'd gotten off the Checker Mill Fire.

She spent most of the hour's hike up his trail telling herself she was being an idiot. A kiss, one bowl of chili, and one fire killed right at the very edge of a vegetable patch. That's all there was between them.

But each day on the fires since, she'd been watching Candace and Luke. And each time she thought about the second kiss, the one after the fire—the more she knew that she at least had to answer the question that she and Colin had written between them.

The climb to his cabin followed a fast-running stream and then stretched out over a long green meadow. The fire had been killed in the woods. The last lines of trees stood green as well except for some char on the bark. For once, the fire's story had gone exactly as she'd predicted it.

His kiss had been a place of peace that had felt so right, so perfect. Part of it was the land, most of it was the man. The last of it was that he was the sort of man who had chosen this gorgeous stretch of mountainside for himself.

But how would he react to her arrival? Was he just being so thankful to be rescued from the fire that he'd have invited Medusa to come visit?

It had taken her a week after the Checker Mill Fire to make the mental connection. Tori had pulled one of Colin Steele's thrillers off her own bookshelf to discover that the man pictured on the back had introduced himself to her as Colin James.

And that had almost kept her away.

She didn't want to arrive as some sycophant, fan-girl no matter how much she enjoyed his novels. Yet here she was anyway, despite telling herself to stay away.

Tori almost turned from his front porch and headed back down the trail, which was beyond stupid. She closed her eyes, trudged up the steps, and struck out at the door.

There.

Now she'd knocked and there was no backing away without looking even beyond stupider than she felt. Stupiderist? Even by Ginger standards, this was extreme.

And she kept standing there.

And standing there.

She knocked again, harder.

Still nothing.

Well, she hadn't driven and hiked and nerved herself up to quit so easily. *Perseverance,* she reminded herself and stalked off to the back side of the cabin.

10

Colin looked up the moment she came into view. It was like that utterly impossible moment that always occurred between hero and heroine that he could never resist writing. First sight of each other at the same instant.

Even without the fire gear, he'd know her anywhere. There was a confidence, a surety to her stride unlike any other woman he'd ever known, or written. She came around the corner of his cabin as if she'd always been there, always belonged.

He stayed where he was and waited while she crossed the back porch, shed her pack, and came up into the vegetable garden. She wore hiking boots, shorts atop some of the longest legs he'd ever seen, and a light t-shirt luridly aflame, but patterned like a checker board. Across her chest it announced the Checker Mill Fire and the dates. The second date was the last time he'd seen her; twenty days and three hours.

His gaze finally made it up to her eyes as she arrived in front him.

"Great t-shirt."

"I brought one for you. You worked it too."

"Is that why you're here?"

"No. Nor is it that I know who you are."

Colin froze. Here it comes. All of the fantasy and hopes had just become meaningless.

"I've read a lot of your books. I thought you should know. I almost stayed away because of that."

"You what?" He hadn't expected that. "Then why are you here?"

She reached out and brushed her fingertips along his cheek. Not hot like fire, but rather cool like his stream, a caress that calmed and anchored him in this moment.

"You feel it too, don't you?" Tori asked softly.

He could only nod.

She closed the final step that separated them. When she slid her arms around his neck and kissed him, it was a scene right out of fiction. He'd never imagined anyone feeling so right in his arms.

Colin knew that Tori Ellison never stopped once she found what she wanted. She'd keep right on fighting fire or whatever came next in her life just as he'd always be writing.

When they lay down together on the garden path, he knew that he needed her as much as the blank page needed words. And their story would have many, many pages.

About the Author

M. L. Buchman has over 40 novels in print. His military romantic suspense books have been named Barnes & Noble and NPR "Top 5 of the year" and Booklist "Top 10 of the Year." He has been nominated for the Reviewer's Choice Award for "Top 10 Romantic Suspense of 2014" by RT Book Reviews. In addition to romance, he also writes thrillers, fantasy, and science fiction.

In among his career as a corporate project manager he has: rebuilt and single-handed a fifty-foot sailboat, both flown and jumped out of airplanes, designed and built two houses, and bicycled solo around the world.

He is now making his living as a full-time writer on the Oregon Coast with his beloved wife. He is constantly amazed at what you can do with a degree in Geophysics. You may keep up with his writing by subscribing to his newsletter at: www.mlbuchman.com.

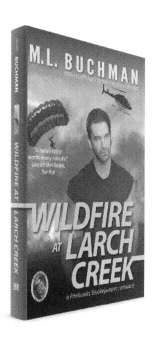

Wildfire at Larch Creek
(a Firehawks romance excerpt)

Two-Tall Tim Harada leaned over Akbar the Great's shoulder to look out the rear door of the DC-3 airplane.

"Ugly," he shouted over the roar of the engine and wind.

Akbar nodded rather than trying to speak.

Since ugly was their day job, it didn't bother Tim much, but this was worse than usual. It would be their fourth smokejump in nine days on the same fire. The Cottonwood Peak Fire was being a total pain in the butt, even worse than usual for a wildfire. Every time they blocked it in one direction, the swirling winds would turn-about and drive the fire toward a new point on the compass. Typical for the Siskiyou Mountains of northern California, but still a pain.

Akbar tossed out a pair of crepe paper streamers and they watched together. The foot-wide streamers caught wind and curled, loop-the-looped through vortices, and reversed direction at least three times. Pretty much the worst conditions possible for a parachute jump.

"It's what we live for!"

Akbar nodded and Tim didn't have to see his best friend's face to know about the fierce wildness of his white grin on his Indian-dark face. Or the matching one against his own part-Vietnamese coloring. Many women told him that his mixed Viet,

French-Canadian, and Oklahoman blood made him intriguingly exotic—a fact that had never hurt his prospects in the bar.

The two of them were the first-stick smokejumpers for Mount Hood Aviation, the best freelance firefighters of them all. This was—however moronic—*precisely* what they lived for. He'd followed Akbar the Great's lead for five years and the two of them had climbed right to the top.

"Race you," Akbar shouted then got on the radio and called directions about the best line of attack to "DC"—who earned his nickname from his initials matching the DC-3 jump plane he piloted.

Tim moved to give the deployment plan to the other five sticks still waiting on their seats; no need to double check it with Akbar, the best approach was obvious. Heck, this was the top crew. The other smokies barely needed the briefing; they'd all been watching through their windows as the streamers cavorted in the chaotic winds.

Then, while DC turned to pass back over the jump zone, he and Akbar checked each others' gear. Hard hat with heavy mesh face shield, Nomex fire suit tight at the throat, cinched at the waist, and tucked in the boots. Parachute and reserve properly buckled, with the static line clipped to the wire above the DC-3's jump door. Pulaski fire axe, fire shelter, personal gear bag, chain saw on a long rope tether, gas can…the list went on, and through long practice took them under ten seconds to verify.

Five years they'd been jumping together, the last two as lead stick. Tim's body ached, his head swam with fatigue, and he was already hungry though they'd just eaten a full meal at base camp and a couple energy bars on the short flight back to the fire. All the symptoms were typical for a long fire.

DC called them on close approach. Once more Akbar leaned out the door, staying low enough for Tim to lean out over him. Not too tough as Akbar was a total shrimp and Tim had earned the "Two-Tall" nickname for being two Akbars tall. He wasn't called Akbar the Great for his height, but rather for his powerful build and unstoppable energy on the fire line.

"Let's get it done and…" Tim shouted in Akbar's ear as they approached the jump point.

"…come home to Mama!" and Akbar was gone.

Tim actually hesitated before launching himself after Akbar and ended up a hundred yards behind him.

Come home to Mama? Akbar had always finished the line, *Go get the girls.* Ever since the wedding, Akbar had gotten all weird in the head. Just because he was married and happy was no excuse to—

The static line yanked his chute. He dropped below the tail of the DC-3—always felt as if he had to duck, but doorways on the ground did the same thing to him—and the chute caught air and jerked him hard in the groin.

The smoke washed across the sky. High, thin cirrus clouds promised an incoming weather change, but wasn't going to help them much today. The sun was still pounding the wilderness below with a scorching, desiccating heat that turned trees into firebrands at a single spark.

The Cottonwood Peak Fire was chewing across some hellacious terrain. Hillsides so steep that some places you needed mountaineering gear to go chase the flames. Hundred-and-fifty foot Doug firs popping off like fireworks. Ninety-six thousand acres, seventy percent contained and a fire as angry as could be that they were beating it down.

Tim yanked on the parachute's control lines as the winds caught him and tried to fling him back upward into the sky. On a jump like this you spent as much time making sure that the chute didn't tangle with itself in the chaotic winds as you did trying to land somewhere reasonable.

Akbar had called it right though. They had to hit high on this ridge and hold it. If not, that uncontained thirty percent of the wildfire was going to light up a whole new valley to the east and the residents of Hornbrook, California were going to have a really bad day.

His chute spun him around to face west toward the heart of the blaze. Whoever had rated this as seventy percent contained clearly needed his head examined. Whole hillsides were still alight with flame. It was only because the MHA smokies had cut so many firebreaks over the last eight days, combined with the constant pounding of the big Firehawk helicopters dumping retardant loads every which way, that the whole mountain range wasn't on fire.

Tim spotted Akbar. Below and to the north. Damn but that guy could fly a chute. Tim dove hard after him.

Come home to Mama! Yeesh! But the dog had also found the perfect lady. Laura Jenson: wilderness guide, expert horse-woman—who was still trying to get Tim up on one of her beasts—and who was really good for Akbar. But it was as if Tim no longer recognized his best friend.

They used to crawl out of a fire, sack out in the bunks for sixteen-straight, then go hit the bars. *What do I do for a living? I parachute out of airplanes to fight wildfires by hand.* It wowed the women every time, gained them pick of the crop.

Now when Akbar hit the ground, Laura would be waiting in her truck and they'd

disappear to her little cabin in the woods.
What was up with that anyway?

Tim looked down and cursed. He
should have been paying more attention.
Akbar was headed right into the center
of the only decent clearing, and Tim was
on the verge of overflying the ridge and
landing in the next county.

He yanked hard on the right control of
his chute, swung in a wide arc, and prayed
that the wind gods would be favorable just
this once. They were, by inches. Instead
of smacking face first into the drooping
top of a hemlock that he hadn't seen
coming, he swirled around it, receiving
only a breath-stealing slap to the ribs, and
dropped in close beside Akbar.

"Akbar the Great rules!"

His friend demanded a high five for
making a cleaner landing than Tim's before
he began stuffing away his chute.

In two minutes, the chutes were in
their stuff bags and they'd shifted over
to firefighting mode. The next two sticks
dropped into the space they'd just vacated.
Krista nailed her landing more cleanly than

Tim or Akbar had. Jackson ate an aspen,
but it was only a little one, so he was on the
ground just fine, but he had to cut down
the tree to recover his chute. Didn't matter;
they had to clear the whole ridge anyway—
except everyone now had an excuse to tease
him.

# # #

Forty hours later Tim had spent thirty
hours non-stop on the line and ten crashed
face first into his bunk. Those first thirty
had been a grueling battle of clearing the
ridgeline and scraping the earth down to
mineral soils. The heat had been obscene as
the fire climbed the face of the ridge, rising
until it had towered over them in a wall of
raging orange and thick, smoke-swirl black
a couple dozen stories high.

The glossy black-and-racing-flame
painted dots of the MHA Firehawks had
looked insignificant as they dove, dropping
eight tons of bright-red retardant alongside
the fire or a thousand gallons of water
directly on the flames as called for. The
smaller MD500s were on near-continuous

call-up to douse hotspots where sparks had jumped the line. Emily, Jeannie, and Vern, their three night-drop certified pilots, had flown right through the night to help them kill it. Mickey and the others picking it back up at daybreak.

Twice they'd been within minutes of having to run and once they were within seconds of deploying their fire shelters, but they'd managed to beat it back each time. There was a reason that smokejumpers were called on a Type I wildfire incident. They delivered. And the Mount Hood Aviation smokies had a reputation of being the best in the business; they'd delivered on that as well.

Tim had hammered face down into his bunk, too damn exhausted to shower first. Which meant his sheets were now char-smeared and he'd have to do a load of laundry. He jumped down out of the top bunk, shifting sideways to not land on Akbar if he swung out of the lower bunk at the same moment…except he wasn't there. His sheets were neat and clean, the blanket tucked in. Tim's were the only set of boots on the tiny bit of floor the two of them usually jostled for. Akbar now stayed overnight in the bunkhouse only if Laura was out on a wilderness tour ride with her horses.

Tim thought about swapping his sheets for Akbar's clean ones, but it hardly seemed worth the effort.

Following tradition, Tim went down the hall, kicking the doors and receiving back curses from the crashed-out smokies. The MHA base camp had been a summer camp for Boy Scouts or something way too many years ago. The halls were narrow and the doors thin.

"Doghouse!" he hollered as he went. He raised a fist to pound on Krista's door when a voice shouted from behind it.

"You do that, Harada, and I'm gonna squish your tall ass down to Akbar's runt size."

That was of course a challenge and he beat on her door with a quick rattle of both fists before sprinting for the safety of the men's showers.

Relative safety.

He was all soaped up in the doorless plywood shower stall, when a bucket of ice-cold water blasted him back against the wall.

He yelped! He couldn't help himself. She must have dipped it from the glacier-fed stream that ran behind the camp it was so freaking cold.

Her raucous laugh said that maybe she had.

He considered that turnabout might be fair play, but with Krista you never knew. If he hooked up a one-and-a-half inch fire hose, she might get even with a three hundred-gallon helicopter drop. And then… Maybe he'd just shame her into buying the first round at the Doghouse Inn.

Tim resoaped and scrubbed and knew he'd still missed some patches of black. The steel sheets attached to the wall as mirrors were as useless now as they'd been before decades of Boy Scouts had tried to carve their initials into them. Usually he and Akbar checked each other because you ended up with smoke or char stains in the strangest spots.

But Akbar wasn't here.

Tim didn't dare wait for any of the others. If he was caught still in the shower by all the folks he'd just rousted from their sacks, it wouldn't turn out well.

He made it back to his room in one piece. The guys who'd showered last night were already on their way out. Good, they'd grab the table before he got down into town and hit the Doghouse Inn. The grimy ones weren't moving very fast yet.

Tim had slept through breakfast and after the extreme workout of a long fire his stomach was being pretty grouchy about that.

# # #

As Macy Tyler prepared for it, she regretted saying yes to a date with Brett Harrison. She regretted not breaking the date the second after she'd made it. And she hoped that by the time the evening with Brett Harrison was over she wouldn't regret not dying of some exotic Peruvian parrot flu earlier in the day.

Just because they'd both lived in Larch Creek, Alaska their entire lives was not reason enough for her to totally come apart. Was it?

Actually it was nothing against Brett particularly. But she knew she was still borderline psychotic about men. It was her first date since punching out her fiancé on the altar, and the intervening six months had not been sufficient for her to be completely rational on the subject.

After fussing for fifteen minutes, she gave herself up as a lost cause. Macy hanked her dark, dead straight, can't-do-crap-with-it hair back in a long ponytail, put on a bra just because—it was mostly optional with her build, and pulled on a t-shirt. Headed for the door, she caught sight of herself in the hall mirror and saw which t-shirt she'd grabbed: *Helicopter Pilots Get It Up Faster.*

She raced back to her bedroom and switched it out for: *People Fly Airplanes, Pilots* Fly Helicopters. And knocked apart her ponytail in the process. Hearing Brett's pickup on the gravel street, she left her hair down, grabbed a denim jacket, and headed for the door.

Macy hurried out and didn't give Brett time to climb down and open the door of his rattletrap Ford truck for her, if he'd even thought of it.

"Look nice, Macy," was all the greeting he managed which made her feel a little better about the state of her own nerves.

He drove into town, which was actually a bit ridiculous, but he'd insisted he would pick her up. Town was four blocks long and she only lived six blocks from the center of it. They rolled down Buck Street, up Spitz Lane, and down Dave Court to Jack London Avenue—which had the grandest name but was only two blocks long because of a washout at one end and the back of the pharmacy-gas station at the other.

This north side of town was simply "The Call" because all of the streets were named for characters from *The Call of the Wild.* French Pete and Jack London had sailed the Alaskan seaways together. So, as streets were added, the founders had made sure they were named after various of London's books. Those who lived in "The Fang" to the south were stuck with charac-

ters from White Fang for their addresses
including: Grey Beaver Boulevard, Weedon
Way, and Lip-lip Lane.

Macy wished that she and French
Pete's mate Hilma—he went on to marry
an Englishwoman long after he'd left and
probably forgotten Larch Creek—hadn't
been separated by a century of time; the
woman must have really been something.

Macy tried to start a conversation with
Brett, but rapidly discovered that she'd
forgotten to bring her brain along on this
date and couldn't think of a thing to say.

They hit the main street at the foot of
Hal's Folly—the street was only the length
of the gas station, named for the idiot who
drove a dogsled over thin ice and died for
it in London's book. It was pure irony that
the street was short and steep. When it
was icy, the Folly could send you shooting
across the town's main street and off into
Larch Creek—which was much more of a
river than a creek. The street froze in early
October, but the river was active enough
that you didn't want to go skidding out
onto the ice before mid-November.

Brett drove them up past the contradictory storefronts which were all on the "high side" of the road—the "low side" and occasionally the road itself disappeared for a time during the spring floods. The problem was that almost all of the buildings were from the turn of the century, but half were from the turn of this century and half were from the turn before. The town had languished during the 1900s and only experienced a rebirth over the last four decades.

Macy kept her attention on the town so that she didn't have to freak herself out by looking at Brett.

Old log cabins and modern stick-framed buildings with generous windows stood side by side. Mason's Galleria was an ultra-modern building of oddly-shaded glass and no right angles. One of the town mysteries was how Mason kept the art gallery in business when Larch Creek attracted so few tourists. Macy's favorite suggestion was that the woman—who was always dressed in the sharpest New York clothes and spoke so fast that no one could understand her—

was actually a front for the Alaskan mafia
come to rule Larch Creek.

This newest, most modern building in
town was tight beside the oldest and dark-
est structure.

French Pete's, where Brett parked
his truck, was the anchor at the center
of town and glowered out at all of the
other structures. The heavy-log, two-story
building dominated Parisian Way—as the
main street of Larch Creek was named by
the crazy French prospector who founded
the town in the late-1800s. He'd named the
trading post after himself and the town
after the distinctive trees that painted the
surrounding hills yellow every fall. French
Pete had moved on, but a Tlingit woman
he'd brought with him stayed and bore him
a son after his departure. It was Hilma who
had made sure the town thrived.

There had been a recent upstart
movement to rename the town because
having the town of Larch Creek *on*
Larch Creek kept confusing things. "Rive
Gauche" was the current favorite during
heavy drinking at French Pete's because

the town was on the "left bank" of Larch
Creek. If you were driving in on the only
road, the whole town was on the left bank;
like the heart of Paris. The change had
never made it past the drinking stage, so
most folk just ignored the whole topic, but
it persisted on late Saturday nights.

Macy took strength from the town. She
had loved it since her first memories. And
just because she'd been dumb enough to
agree to a date with Brett, she wasn't going
to blame Larch Creek for that.

Well, not much. Perhaps, if there were
more than five hundred folk this side of
Liga Pass, there would be a single man that
she could date who didn't know every detail
of her life. She still clung onto the idea that
she'd find a decent man somewhere among
the chaff.

Dreamer!

That wasn't entirely fair. After all, some
of them, like Brett, were decent enough.

The problem was that she, in turn, knew
every detail of their lives. Macy had gone
to school with each of them for too many
years and knew them all too well. A lot

of her classmates left at a dead run after graduation and were now up in Fairbanks, though very few went further afield. The thirty-mile trip back to Larch Creek from "the city" might as well be three hundred for how often they visited. The first half of the trip was on Interstate 4 which was kept open year round. But once you left the main highway, the road narrowed and twisted ten miles over Liga Pass with harsh hairpins and little forgiveness. It didn't help that it was closed as often as it was open in the winter months. The last five miles were through the valley's broad bottom land.

The town was four blocks long from the Unitarian church, which was still a movie theater on Friday and Saturday nights, at the north end of town to the grange at the south end. The houses crawled up the hills to the east. And the west side of the fast-running, glacier-fed river, where the forested hills rose in an abrupt escarpment, belonged to bear, elk, and wolf. Only Old Man Parker had a place on that side, unable to cross during fall freeze-up or spring melt-out. But he and his girlfriend didn't come into town much even when the way was open across running water or thick ice.

The main road ran north to meet the highway to Fairbanks, and in the other direction ended five miles south at Tena. Tena simply meant "trail" in the Tanana dialect and added another couple dozen families to the area. The foot trail out of Tena lead straight toward the massif of Denali's twenty-thousand foot peak which made the valley into a picture postcard.

Macy did her best to draw strength from the valley and mountain during the short drive to French Pete's. Once they hit Parisian Way, a bit of her brain returned. She even managed a polite inquiry about Brett's construction business and was pretty pleased at having done so. Thankfully they were close, so his answer was kept brief.

"Mostly it's about shoring up people's homes before winter hits. There are only a couple new homes a year and Danny gets most of those." He sounded bitter, it was a rivalry that went back to the senior prom and Cheryl Dahl, the prettiest Tanana girl in town.

The fact that Brett and Danny drank together most Saturdays and Cheryl had married Mike Nichol—the one she'd accompanied to the prom—and had three equally beautiful children in Anchorage had done nothing to ease their epic rivalry.

Or perhaps it was because Brett's blue pickup had a bumper sticker that said *America Is Under Construction* and Danny's blue truck had a drawing of his blue bulldozer that read *Vogon Constructor Fleet— specialist in BIG jobs.*

"Small towns," Macy said in the best sympathetic tone she could muster. It was difficult to not laugh in his face, because it was *so* small-town of them.

"This place looks wackier every time," they'd stopped in front of French Pete's. "Carl has definitely changed something, just can't pick it out."

Macy looked up in surprise. The combined bar and restaurant appeared no different to her. Big dark logs made a structure two-stories high with a steep roof to shed the snow. A half dozen broad steps led up to a deep porch that had no

room for humans; it was jammed with Carl
Deville's collection of "stuff."

"Your junk. My stuff," Carl would
always say when teased about it by some
unwary tourist. After such an unthinking
comment, they were then as likely to find
horseradish in their turkey sandwich as not.

There was the broken Iditarod sled
from Vic Hornbeck's failed race bid in the
late 1970s piled high with dropped elk ant-
lers. An Elks Lodge hat from Poughkeepsie,
New York still hung over one handle of
the sled. The vintage motorcycle of the
guy who had come through on his way to
solo climb up Denali from the north along
Muldrow Glacier and descend to the south
by Cassin Ridge was still there, buried
under eleven years of detritus. Whether he
made the crossing and didn't come back or
died on the mountain, no one ever knew.

"Man asked me to hold it for him a
bit," Carl would offer in his deep laconic
style when asked by some local teen who
lusted after the wheels. "Don't see no need
to hustle it out from under him. 'Sides, the
baby girl he left in Carol Swenson's belly

whilst he was here is ten now. Mayhaps she'll want it at sixteen."

There was an old wooden lobster pot— that Macy had never understood because the Gulf of Alaska to the south wasn't all that much closer than the Beaufort Sea to the north and the pot looked like it was from Maine—with a garden gnome-sized bare-breasted hula dancer standing inside it; her ceramic paint worn to a patina by too many Alaskan winters spent topless and out of doors. A hundred other objects were scattered about including worn-out gold panning equipment, a couple of plastic river kayaks with "For Rent" signs that might have once been green and sky blue before the sun leached out all color— though she'd never seen them move. And propped in the corner was the wooden propeller from Macy's first plane that she'd snapped when her wheel had caught in an early hole in the permafrost up near Nenana. That was before she'd switched to helicopters. She'd spent a week there before someone could fly in a replacement.

"Looks the same to me."

Brett eyed her strangely as he held open the door.

And just like that she knew she'd blown what little hope this date had right out of the water. Brett had been trying to make conversation and she'd done her true-false test. It wasn't like she was anal, it was more like everyone simply treated her as if she was.

Inside was dark, warm, and just as cluttered. A century or more of oddbits had been tacked to the walls: old photos, snowshoes strung with elk hide, a rusted circular blade several feet across from the old sawmill that had closed back in the sixties, and endless other bits and pieces that Carl and his predecessors had gathered. He claimed direct lineage back to French Pete Deville, through Hilma. It wasn't hard to believe; Carl looked like he'd been born behind the bar. Looked like he might die there too.

The fiction section of the town library lined one long wall of French Pete's. Most of the non-fiction was down at the general store except for religion, movies, and anything to do with mechanics. They were down in the movie house-church's lobby, the mechanical guides because the pharmacy-gas station was next door.

Though Carl didn't have any kin, Natalie, the ten-year-old daughter of Carol Swenson and the mountain climber with the left-behind motorcycle, was sitting up on a high barstool playing chess against Carl. It was a place she could be found most days when there wasn't school and Carol was busy over at the general store and post office. She was such a fixture that over the last few years everyone had pretty much come to expect Natty to take over French Pete's someday.

Macy scanned the tables hoping that no one would recognize her, fat chance in a community the size of Larch Creek.

And then she spotted the big table back in the corner beneath the moose-antler chandelier. It was packed.

Oh crap! She'd forgotten it was Sunday.

Too late to run for cover, she guided Brett in the other direction to a table in the corner. She managed to sit with her back to her father's expression of mock horror. That she could deal with.

But it would have been easier if Mom hadn't offered a smile and a wink.

Available at fine retailers everywhere

More information at:
www.mlbuchman.com

Other works by M.L. Buchman

Where Dreams Reside
Maria's Christmas Table
Where Dreams Unfold
Where Dreams Are Written

Dieties Anonymous
Cookbook from Hell: Reheated
Saviors 101

Thrillers
Swap Out!
One Chef!
Two Chef!

SF/F Titles
Nara
Monk's Maze

Printed in Great Britain
by Amazon